SEE THE MAP IN THIS BOOK
COME ALIVE!

1. Download the free **AR Reads** app on your Android- or iOS-compatible smartphone or tablet.

2. Launch the app and hover your device over the map to explore Flynn and Paddy's interactive world. See and hear dragons fly, fire crackle, and get a glimpse of your favorite characters in action!

THE DRAGON HUNTERS

A Dragon Brothers Book

James Russell
Link Choi

sourcebooks
jabberwocky

Away across the oceans,
where few have dared to roam,
upon a wondrous island,
a family made its home.

Two brothers, Flynn and Paddy.
Their parents, Mom and Dad.
A lovely dog named Coco,
their chocolate-colored Lab.

One day when it was raining,
the boys were stuck inside.
Paddy thought he'd try to take
poor Coco for a ride.

The dog, she leaped and bucked him off
then tore around the room.
Their mother chased her from the house,
while brandishing her broom.

The boys peered out the window
at Coco's sad wee face,
when a sudden, swooping dragon
left nothing in her place!

"A dragon stole our dog!"
the boys cried out together.
"Please stop telling tales," said Mom,
"and pray for better weather."

The boys devised a plan that night
and packed their bags with care.
They swore that by tomorrow
they would find the dragon's lair.

Their mother woke and saw them gone.
Said she, "I have a hunch:
they've gone to look for Coco.
At least they took some lunch."

Indeed they had, and by midday
the boys had stopped to rest.
They nibbled on a sandwich—
roast beef with lemon zest.

"I've tasted better sandwiches,"
said Paddy to his brother.
"I know," said Flynn, "I just can't seem
to make them like our mother."

"Come on," said Flynn, "we must attempt
to find our dog today.
I've no idea if she's nearby
or if she's miles away."

Suddenly, upon the breeze,
they heard a mighty roar
followed by the faintest *woof*—
from Coco, they were sure.

Almost at the mountain's peak,
the boys could see a cave.
"I wonder if she's there," said Flynn,
while trying to be brave.

For hours they climbed the mountain,
up a steep and rocky trail.
And when they found the cave at last,
they saw the dragon's tail!

Said Flynn, "Wait here, while I go in
and take a look around.
Make sure you stay invisible.
Try not to make a sound."

Although the dragon was asleep,
that did not make it easy.
The thought of sneaking by those teeth
made Flynn feel mighty queasy.

Meanwhile, outside, all alone,
Paddy was losing hope.
At least until inside his bag,
he found a length of rope.

Creeping past the dragon's nose,
Flynn peered into the dark.
Coco, his beloved dog,
was just about to bark!

"Shhhh," he said to keep her quiet
(a tactic bound to fail).
She barked and leaped and leaped and barked
and wagged her waggly tail.

The dragon gave a fearsome roar
and Flynn began to run.
"Come on!" he yelled to Coco,
who thought it was great fun.

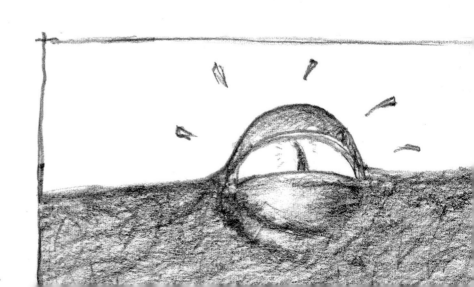

Flynn grabbed ahold of Paddy's hand
as he scampered past.
"We have to be extremely brave
and run extremely fast!"

The chasing dragon came so close
it thought, "I've nearly got 'em!"
Paddy felt its fiery breath
warming up his bottom.

As the dragon lunged to bite
poor Paddy's derriere,
to its surprise it chomped upon
a mouthful of fresh air.

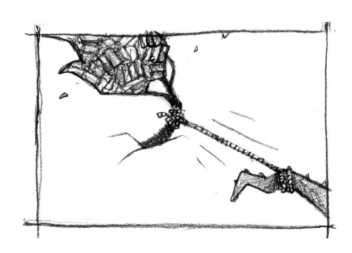

Now, never underestimate
a boy's ability.
For with his rope the lad had tied
the dragon to a tree.

Just as dusk was falling,
the boys arrived back home.
"Dinner!" called their mother.
"And for Coco I've a bone."

Said Flynn, "We beat the dragon—
rescued Coco from her fate."
Said Mom, "That's nice, my darlings.
Now off to bed. It's late!"

The boys were quickly snoring and
in sleep they did succumb
to dreams of chasing dragons
and adventures yet to come.

THE END

Published by Sourcebooks Jabberwocky, an imprint of Sourcebooks, Inc.
P.O. Box 4410, Naperville, Illinois 60567-4410
(630) 961-3900
Fax: (630) 961-2168
www.sourcebooks.com

Originally published in 2012 in New Zealand by Dragon Brothers Ltd.

Library of Congress Cataloging-in-Publication data is on file with the publisher.

Source of Production: Leo Paper, Heshan City, Guangdong Province, China
Date of Production: January 2017
Run Number: 5008066

Printed and bound in China.
LEO 10 9 8 7 6 5 4 3 2 1

For my own dragon boys

—JR

For Alice and Martin, who drew
the scariest cats.

—LC

The Dragon Hunters is the first book of
The Dragon Brothers Trilogy. To find out more about
Flynn and Paddy's world visit www.dragonbrothersbooks.com.

THE ADVENTURE CONTINUES!

Be on the lookout for books 2 and 3 in the Dragon Brothers series!

THE DRAGON TAMERS

coming June 2017

When Flynn and Paddy discover a strange map that shows magical-sounding landmarks all around their island home, they decide it's time to go exploring! But when they unexpectedly stumble across a dragon hatchery, the brothers end up going home with more than an epic story...

THE DRAGON RIDERS

coming August 2017

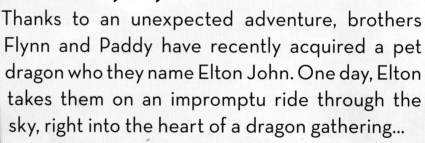

Thanks to an unexpected adventure, brothers Flynn and Paddy have recently acquired a pet dragon who they name Elton John. One day, Elton takes them on an impromptu ride through the sky, right into the heart of a dragon gathering...

EXPERIENCE THE MAGIC—IN 3D!

You've read the story; now watch it unfold before your eyes! Join the dragons and soar above Flynn and Paddy's magical island home as your imagination comes to life! Cutting-edge augmented reality technology brings their world off the page and into yours. All it takes is **two simple steps:**

1. Download the free AR Reads app on your Android- or iOS-compatible smartphone or tablet.

2. Launch the app and hover your device over the map to explore Flynn and Paddy's interactive world. See and hear dragons fly, fire crackle, and get a glimpse of your favorite characters in action!

Don't have a smartphone or tablet? Visit **dragonbrothersbooks .com/blog** to watch a video on how the augmented reality works.

About the Author and Illustrator

James Russell, an author and journalist from New Zealand, was blessed to spend his childhood holidaying in the wilderness—from the coast, to the pristine inland lakes, to the towering mountain ranges of the South Island.

It's those majestic and mystical places, their flora and fauna, and the sense of adventure he felt in exploring them that form the backdrop of much of his writing today.

Inspiration also comes from observing the humor, imagination, and carefree spirit of his own two young boys as they discover the natural world around them. He is married to Rebecca and lives in Auckland.

Link Choi was a finalist for the Russell Clark Medal for Illustration for his work on *The Dragon Hunters*. When he is not reading or making picture books, he helps create the look of films such as the Hobbit trilogy. He lives in Auckland, New Zealand.

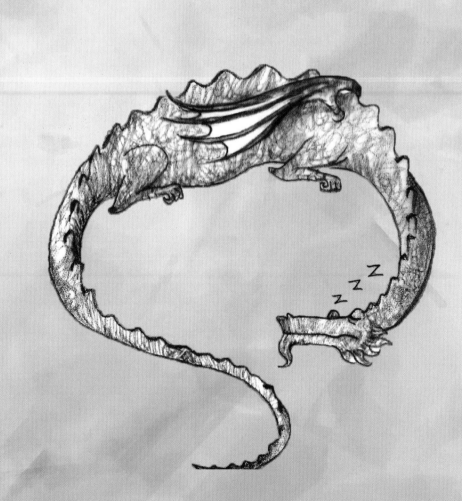

DRAGON HATCHERY
DRAGON'S LAIR
MT. MONSTROUS
RIDGE OF RISING FLAME
SWAMP OF CHILDREN'S WISHES
TREE OF WAILING WITCHES
RICKETY TRAIL
MEADOW OF DREAMS
ANCIENT FOREST
FLYNN & PADDY'S HOUSE
MYSTIC MO
N
E
W
S